MIDLOTHIAN PUBLIC LIBRARY
[redacted]
3 1614 0018
W9-BIU-795

Woof & Quack in Winter

MIDLOTHIAN PUBLIC LIBRARY
14701 S. KENTON AVENUE
MIDLOTHIAN, IL 60445

For new friends and true friends. —J.A.S.

To my parents, Jim & Jean, who let me be myself. —R.S.

E
SWE

Text copyright © 2017 by Jamie A. Swenson
Illustrations copyright © 2017 by Ryan Sias

First Green Light Readers edition 2017

All rights reserved. Green Light Readers® and its logo are trademarks of HMH Publishers LLC, registered in the United States and other countries.

For information about permission to reproduce selections from this book, write to trade.permissions@hmhco.com or to Permissions, Houghton Mifflin Harcourt Publishing Company, 3 Park Avenue, 19th Floor, New York, New York 10016.

www.hmhco.com
The text of this book is set in ITC Lubalin Graph Std.
The display type is set in ITC Lubalin Graph Std.

Library of Congress Cataloging-in-Publication Data is on file.

ISBN: 978-0-544-95949-1 paper over board
ISBN: 978-0-544-95902-6 paperback

Manufactured in China
SCP 10 9 8 7 6 5 4 3 2 1
4500661230

Woof & Quack in Winter

by Jamie A. Swenson
illustrated by Ryan Sias

Houghton Mifflin Harcourt
Boston New York

Woof, I am not flying south this year.

But ducks always fly south, Quack.

I want to stay with you in winter.
This duck is staying put.
It will be too cold for you.
You do not have fur.

I have fluffy down.
Not on your feet. You will have cold feet.
I will not have cold feet. I will stay with you.

So Quack did not fly south.
Snow started falling.

Snow covered everything.

Where is the grass?
Under the snow.

Where is my pond?
Under the ice.

Where are my feet?
Under the snow.

Winter is too cold for ducks.
BRRrrrrr!
No, I want to play in the snow!

Woof and Quack went sledding.

Woof and Quack made a snow duck.

Woof and Quack went ice skating.

BRRrrrrr!
Winter is fun. I am glad I stayed put.
I am glad you are here too. But this dog wants to fly south.
SHIVER
SHIVER

Dogs do not fly south in the winter.
This dog is flying south!

So Woof and Quack flew south.

Woof and Quack went sledding.

Woof and Quack made a sand dog.

Woof and Quack went swimming.

Winter snow is fun,
but so is winter sun.

Winter friends are best of all.